Mama, Across the Sea

For Laura,

Elodie,

and the others . . .

children from here to there

Henry Holt and Company, LLC, *Publishers since 1866*
115 West 18th Street, New York, New York 10011
Henry Holt is a registered trademark of Henry Holt and Company, LLC
Copyright © 1998 by Albin Michel Jeunesse
Translation copyright © 2000 by Henry Holt and Company
All rights reserved. First published in the United States in 1999 by Henry Holt and Company.
Published in Canada by Fitzhenry & Whiteside Ltd., 195 Allstate Parkway, Markham, Ontario L3R 4T8.
Originally published in France in 1998 by Albin Michel Jeunesse under the title *Maman-dlo*.

Library of Congress Cataloging-in-Publication Data
Godard, Alex. [Maman-dlo. English]
Mama, across the sea / Alex Godard; adapted from the French by George Wen.
Summary: Although she loves the sunny island where she lives
with her grandparents, Cecile longs to see her mother again.
[1. Grandmother—Fiction. 2. Caribbean Area—Fiction.] I. Wen, George. II. Title.
PZ7.G53885Mam 1999 [E]—dc21 99-10098

ISBN 0-8050-6161-4
First American Edition—2000
Printed in France

1 3 5 7 9 10 8 6 4 2

Mama, Across the Sea

ALEX GODARD

Adapted from the French by

GEORGE WEN

Henry Holt and Company • New York

It was almost noon.

   The tin roof Cecile sat on was burning hot,
but she didn't care. She was waiting for her mother.

   Suddenly she saw a tiny speck on the horizon. The speck
was moving slowly toward the shore in a trail of white foam.

   "Mama!" cried Cecile.

But it was only Gilles coming back from a day's fishing.

Once on shore, everyone swarmed around Gilles's boat to get a pound of his catch of catfish and parrotfish.

The horizon was now empty. Mama wouldn't be coming today. Cecile would wait again tomorrow.

When Cecile heard her grandma's voice, she tried to sneak down from the roof, but Grandma was there, waiting for her.

"Heavens, Cecile!" Grandma scolded. "How many times have I told you that girls shouldn't be climbing trees, let alone roofs. What would I tell your mother if you got hurt?"

Cecile lowered her head.

Grandma sighed loudly. "Go and get Grandpa. Lunch is ready," she said.

Grandpa was repairing his fishing net in the shade of an almond tree.

"Grandma sent me to get you," Cecile said.

"Uh-huh," Grandpa murmured without looking up.

Cecile sat down to wait for Grandpa to finish. She listened to the sea as it gently clicked and clacked with the sound of shells and pebbles knocking against each other.

Suddenly Cecile had an idea.

She would draw a picture and send it to her mother—a picture that would make her mother want to come home. She'd glue on shells and sand from the beach at Port Royal. The sand there was pink, and it was very, very fine. She wanted to run to Port Royal Beach right then but Grandma was waiting.

After lunch, Grandma and Cecile spent the afternoon papering the walls of the house with colorful pictures cut out of catalogs.

When they finished, they stood by the table admiring how pretty the room looked.

Suddenly, Grandma lifted the corner of the pink tablecloth and pulled out an envelope. "Cecile, can you read this letter for me?" she asked.

Neither Grandma nor Grandpa knew how to read. To help out their parents, they both had to start working when they were very young and so they didn't go to school.

"It's a letter from Social Security," Cecile said. "They want to see you."

"Thank you," her grandma said. "I'll go into town tomorrow morning."

As soon as Grandma left the next morning, Cecile took
the path across the swamp to get to Port Royal. Quickly she
ran along the beach picking out the most beautiful shells
and the best pink sand.

When she got home, Cecile took out a sheet of drawing paper and her colored pencils. What would she draw for Mama?

She drew a turtledove in the sky. Then erased it. It was hard to make a picture for Mama. She had been away a long time. Did Mama still like the same things?

I'll draw the sky, Cecile decided. Mama really needs a blue sky, because where Mama lives, the sky is always gray.

Cecile drew a blue sky, and a wooden shack with a wavy tin roof. In the background, she drew a geiger tree with lots of leaves. Where Mama lives now, trees lose their leaves when it gets cold.

Grandpa says it's very cold there. Cecile imagined people walking around inside a refrigerator, and she drew a big yellow sun.

Then all around her picture Cecile glued on shells: conch shells, zebra-striped shells, iridescent shells shaped like butterflies. And finally she glued sand to her picture. "When Mama sees the sand, she'll want to come home," thought Cecile.

Grandma was unhappy when she got back from town that evening. She had had to pay two people to sign for her so she could cash her pension check.

Cecile didn't like to see her grandma unhappy, so she decided to teach her how to write. She got out an old school notebook and wrote A . . . , B . . . , C. . . . Then she took Grandma's hand in hers, and just like her teacher had done with her, guided her grandma's hand to make the letters.

Suddenly, Grandma burst out laughing. "My letters look like chicken scratches!" she said.

Cecile smiled and hugged her.

The next morning a letter arrived for Cecile from her mama.

April 14

Dear Cecile,

How are you? Everything is fine with me. I've just found a good job. But I do not get any days off for a long time, so I won't be coming to see you this year.

I miss you. Hug and kiss everyone for me.

All my love,

Your Mama, across the sea

Cecile was so unhappy. She would have to wait another year to see her mother.

Slowly Cecile wandered over to the beach. There were a lot of people gathered around Racik, listening to him play his flute. Racik made his flute sing with a deep, soulful sound, like the cooing of a turtledove. It made Cecile feel not so sad anymore.

Racik smiled at Cecile. "A story?" he asked.

Cecile nodded.

"It was dusk," began Racik. "Two brothers were on their way home after a long day's fishing, their stomachs as empty as their boat.

" 'What kind of life is this?' said the younger brother in disgust. 'Days on end tossing about in this old boat and not a single fish!'

" 'True,' said his older brother. 'But remember last month—just as we were ready to give up, our empty nets filled up with more fish than our boat could hold. Just be patient—a little something in your stomach and you'll be thinking about taking the boat out tomorrow!'

"As the hungry brothers debated how to make the best fish stew, they suddenly heard a laugh ricochet off the water: 'Ha!'

" 'What's that?' asked the younger brother.

" 'It's just your stomach growling,' said the older brother.

" 'Ha! Ha! Ha! Ha!'

" 'And that?' the younger brother cried.

" 'Only the wind whips and snaps like that,' replied his brother. But there wasn't even the slightest breeze in the air.

"When the same laugh rolled over the sea for the third time, the two brothers saw a beautiful woman with long black hair riding toward them over the waves on a sea turtle.

" 'Oh, my dear fishermen!' she called out to them in a sweet voice. 'Look what I have for you.'

"Suddenly, before their eyes the dark belly of the sea lit up like the sun.

" 'Come with me and I will fill your boat with gold,' said the woman softly. 'You will never have to wait for fish again!'

"Through the luminous light, the older brother saw silvery fins where the woman's legs should have been.

" 'Don't listen to her, brother! Don't dive!' cried the older one. 'She is a siren!'

"But it was too late. His brother had already jumped into the water.

" 'Ha! Ha! Ha!' chuckled the siren, flipping her fins before disappearing into the sea."

Racik the storyteller picked up his flute and continued, "Day after day, night after night, the fisherman searched for his brother. But it was in vain."

And Racik began to play the deep, soulful tune on his flute again.

That night Cecile thought about Racik's story. A very long time ago, Cecile's father had gone out to sea and he never came back. Every day Mama went to the beach and waited for him to return. But he never did. Then Mama had gone away, too.

Cecile thought about the younger brother in Racik's story. He was tired of waiting—just like her.

Then she thought of the older brother. She was like the older brother, too. Deep down in her heart Cecile knew she would always hope for Mama to come back.

In the mornings Cecile continued to go to the beach to look for Mama's ship. In the afternoons she and Grandma decorated the bedroom with cutouts from catalogs while Grandpa mended the nets. At night Cecile helped Grandma practice writing. And then one morning . . .

June 12

Dear Cecile,

How happy I was to receive your picture. The shells and the sand remind me of walking on Port Royal Beach with you.

I miss you so much that I have made arrangements for you to spend your school vacation here with me! I have so many things to tell you. I will be waiting for you on the landing.

See you soon.

All my love,
Your Mama, across the sea

Cecile could hardly contain her excitement. The day before her departure, she tried to sit patiently as Grandma combed her hair. Then Grandma helped her pack her suitcase. Cecile was ready to go!

The next day Cecile was up with the roosters. She hadn't slept all night.

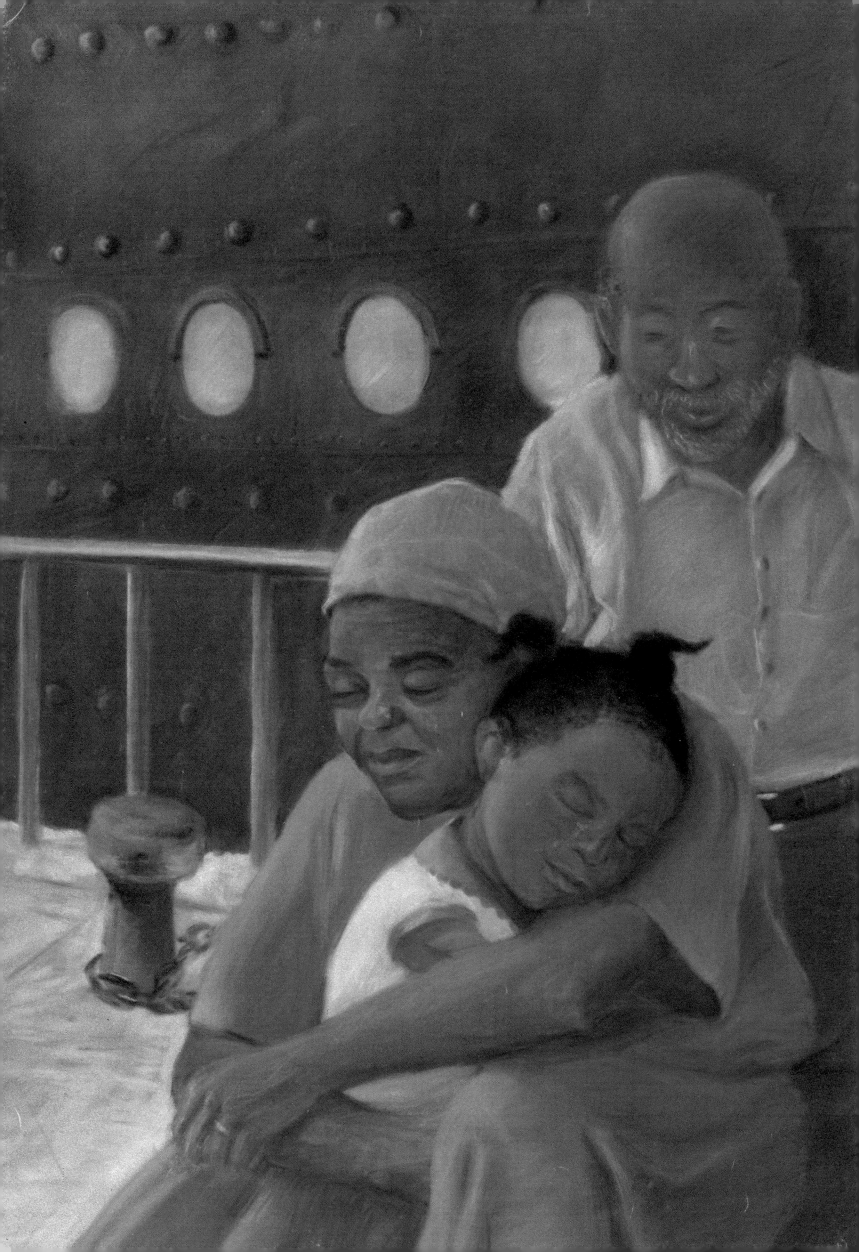

Grandma hugged Cecile close to her chest.

"Come home soon," Grandpa whispered into Cecile's ear.

"Wait for me," said Cecile. "I'll be back. And maybe one day Mama will be back, too."

But for now, Cecile was ready... ready to sail to her Mama, across the sea.